Queer Love And Other Stories

Reading Relaxation Differently

Suparna Roy

Ukiyoto Publishing

All global publishing rights are held by

Ukiyoto Publishing

Published in 2023

Content Copyright © Suparna Roy

ISBN 9789360496746

All rights reserved.
No part of this publication may be reproduced,
transmitted, or stored in a retrieval system, in any
form by any means, electronic, mechanical,
photocopying, recording or otherwise, without the
prior permission of the publisher.

The moral rights of the author have been asserted.

This book is sold subject to the condition that it shall
not by way of trade or otherwise, be lent, resold, hired
out or otherwise circulated, without the publisher's
prior consent, in any form of binding or cover other
than that in which it is published.

www.ukiyoto.com

Dedication

I am intensely grateful to my parents, family, and friends for allowing me to complete this project.

Contents

Krishna/Kanha	1
Duality In Existence!	4
Fascinating Tales: Opting A Bi-Focal Lens	7
Inking And Inspiring!	12
Drizzle-Open!	17
Conversing-Failure	21
Does "Ideal" Exist? - Let's Be Open	25
Society And Humans: A Reflection From Marginalized Perspectives.	31
An Idea On Feminism- Demanded Comment For Generation!	36
Stories From India	41
About the Author	*45*

Krishna/Kanha

The one known for being Loved by All

In English Literature, the branch of it which deals with Queer studies, focuses on the validity of love with all its possibilities. In our society, we often say Love has a language; however, that language is politicized too! If love really has any language then that should be 'freedom'. But I see nothing like that in our society. The fact that our society always functions on strategical binaries of this or that, 'love' has also been reflected in the same. We do not even consider the hues of love, the possibilities of love, and the numerous prospects of expressing it. What I find, are restrictions, categorizations which love if "pure" and which is "impure". What I perceive is idealizing one such expression of love and omitting the rest. That is how dualities have come to operation. Love is culturally a stratified, politicized, molded word which includes no longer the true desire of one's but represents a market of communication without attachment.

Love, a spectrum for me, believes in variety and endorses freedom. If you really love someone you will let that person free. Now, we often say Love has a language; however, that language is politicized too! The fact that our society always functions on strategical binaries of this or that, 'love' has also been reflected in the same. We do not even consider the hues of love, the possibilities of love, and the numerous prospects of expressing it. What I find, are restrictions, categorizations which love if "pure" and which is "impure". What I perceive is idealizing one such expression of love and omitting the rest. That is how dualities have come to operation. Love is culturally a stratified, politicized, molded word which includes many other terms to recognize it. Therefore the question "Is it Love?" is undoubtedly valid and a required voice for the present society, as in the name of the 'Love Veil' people controls, rapes, oppresses, rules, kills, throw acids, sells off humans, and what not. Society will always designate the after slash option for these crimes- "Yes, it is Love!" She loved and married him, where is marital rape? He loved her so he threw acid! The favorite and repeated articulations of our surroundings! Hence, it is important to distinguish whether or not it is love, and the 'question should be raised not romanticization of crimes to be done.

We then have started to identify love with marriage. Now, in the multifarious believe system, my interpretation of love and marriage is highly different from mainstream and my thought is inspired more from my belief in the love of *'Kanha'*. Marriage is a political and patriarchal institution undoubtedly. It is market where two items with required and maintained, accepted and balanced physical and emotional condition are bought and sold. I nowhere, find love existing in marriage. So how my belief in *'Kanha's'* love is-

The love of *'Kanha'* is not bound in marriage,
The love of *'Kanha'* is not bound in rage,
The love of *'Kanha'* is more to feel-
The way we wish our Souls to heal.
Love of *'Kanha'* is very free-
It only needs the inner to perceive,
Love of *'Kanha'* is feminist,
For, it accepts all possibilities of Love that exists.
Bodies in *'Kanha's'* Love does not matter-
It just sees the soul and the fierce desire,
Friendship is also in *'Kanha's'* Love,
Consent has been the beauty of such,
So, if we believe in *'Kanha's'* Love-
Let's embrace the hues of the Souls that may exist in Love!

Duality In Existence!

Tensional forces have levied human beings existences till day. A concept of Absurdism, where we know the futility of our strugglers and yet continue with our endless efforts to find a meaning in these not so meaningful conceptual lives, shows how every shadow can also portray bumming rays of hopefulness. Each human's purpose has always functioned to provide them with a meaning to survive, to combat with turbulences of life. Every format of struggle has something to learn. Either it is a blessing or a lesion, we do not lose anything when we fail or fall into dark vicious circles in our lives. Every time we learn, the pros and cons, as the worst phases of our lives leads to the best avenues to fly high, yes, perhaps, only if we believe we can. Theoretically speaking of which finding a 'moon of shadow', we can always adhere to Albert Camus's The Myth of Sisyphus- where he explained, "The absurdist born out of this confrontation between the human need and the unreasonable silence of the world." Why is it important to believe and try d=searching for a moon in every shadow, because it psychologically nurtures sense of 'need' that will help a person to pursue for repeated targets , even if one is unable to attempt it. A mixture of both jovial and distress happenings constructs the systematic pattern of every breathing beings. So, could you guys find the moon of your shadowy experiences? If not, commence your endeavor once again!

Oscillation indicates the repetitive variation of anything, and justice keeps on varying with time and space, more particularly controlled and influenced by politics and its vulnerably molded devices. Society has emerged with complicated and complex anthropological issues where 'justice' often can be considered as a vital device of measuring an individual's liberty, identity and existence. Nevertheless, recently, many political situations and circumstances does proves 'justice' keeps on propagating further in space, as we know nothing is created out of vacuum! Now, justice is immensely and crucially a labyrinthine issue in our social culture. Justice varies in our culture and its types includes- varying with class, caste, gender, sexuality, power, race, ethnicity, etc. Justice for a rich won't be the same as a poor, justice for a dalit woman won't be the same as a dalit man or even justice for the dalits won't be same the Brahmins. Justice for a Trans-gender won't be the same for a cis-man/woman. Justice varies because it is not the same for a villager/farmer and a business man belonging to the city. Justice indeed varies in every form it can, to be precise 'justice' is made to vary, compelled to alter and benefit depending upon 'power'. If 'justice' is not forcefully 'blinded' then equality will exist, and the authoritative control on the bodies will be out of league. Hence, greater the oscillation clearer chances of control. But the question is- Is it right?

Fascinating Tales: Opting A Bi-Focal Lens

Fascination simply can mean something which relives our subconscious and layered desires. It can provide concrete eclipse to the silent moon's shade. Tales, on the other hand, can mean something which can pass the time, having a flow, inverted with emotionally challenged and mirthful phases. Therefore, Fascinating Tales should be something which should include these variant features to enrich its shades of application. World of Love can be a minuscule representation of such tales, but not just the heteronormative 'love world', rather, a world where possibilities are immensely appreciated. Eyes and Mind/Thoughts and Seeing: A Complementary Friendship! The thought process of a mind is not influenced by what we perceive but rather how we perceive it! However, at the same time, it is crucial to comprehend 'how we' perceive with the ingrained regulated patterns from our childhood to illustrate, how to visualize a male body and how to see the female? We are thought to observe the male body in terms of few stated and popular masculinity while for female bodies in parameters to some established femininity! Right? I have always wondered sharing many instances of my school travels with you; because it is like re-living what you have already lived.

Although, physically going back to the same place seems impossible without time travel, yet, conversing on it enriches the thrilling chills of the moments. Let's brainstorm a bit in an unconventional way of the numerous probable savoir-faire individuals can go through. Not mandatory that all little heads while they travelled to school were enjoying the scenery, or the gossips, or the morning sneak peeking into tiffin boxes to see what Mother gave. No, not all had the same thoughts. I have heard people saying, school life was the best because they made a lot of memories, remembering the scolding of teachers now feels soothing, the ringing of the school bell, the sharing of home-made tiffin, twenty hands jumping into one lunch-box, cleaning the board after the teacher leaves the classroom given sense of superiority, etcetera. But what exactly 'other' little heads thought- some of parents quarrelling, some thinking to earn money by tuitions so that they do not have to ask parents, some thinking the everyday insults of classmates and teachers, and some wondering will they be able to pay this month's fees? So many possibilities of not so enjoying details exist in these little heads. So, when we talk about travelling in school bus/car, lets give a stoppage here too!

This 'trio' has no form; they are fluid in their existence and beauty. It can be felt but can also be seen through action. They are interlinked, interconnected, and mingled interpersonally. Love is culturally a stratified, politicized, molded word which includes many other terms to recognize it. Love, a spectrum for me, believes in variety and endorses freedom. Now, we often say Love has a language; however, that language is politicized too! The fact that our society always functions on strategical binaries of this or that, 'love' has also been reflected in the same. We do not even consider the hues of love, the possibilities of love, and the numerous prospects of expressing it. What I find, are restrictions, categorizations which love if "pure" and which is "impure". What I perceive is idealizing one such expression of love and omitting the rest.

Now, talking about 'Trust', we see our attachment towards someone inclines us to initially think that these people will be the one, around whom we can be secure; however, in majority cases this pattern breaks and we fumble on our trusting people. This growth of the thought that we are most free and contented with them makes us start believing in them with all our advantages and disadvantages, but with time we see, these people are not one to embrace our flaws, rather they involve in correcting, moderating, and rectifying them as per their 'corrective and moral' lens! Then where does trust goes and grows? Let's bring this sphere in discussion sometimes also!

And finally, going to the realm of Friendship, the first impression on the term indicates 'flexibility'! How does it work, if is the next question that arises, we can surely try comprehending it as a spectrum- we can love a friend and not sentimentalize it with 'trust', we can trust a friend and not sentimentalize it with 'love', we can even not do the both- just a formal friend in need without benefits! We can live in with a friend and never feel any strings attached. We can be friends with anybody, at any place and at any time of age and can even walk away without any note left behind for them! The flexibility is up to such extent- where we meet and stay and live without notifications! This trio is never ending; it is a journey without destination. Hence, keep growing!

The role of eyes and its importance therefore commences here. Maybe, since our childhood days we regarded ' lipstick ' as the beautifying accessory of a female identity and not of a male. With experience and eventual unlearning process, we should now learn to discern ' lipstick ' only as an agent to enhance the beauty and not inherently linked any gender attributes. Eyes are indeed important in a living beings' body, because if we start to commute the way we use our Eyes to observe the world then we can move beyond the understanding of

authenticity/centre/ main and learn to recognize the shades. The way we reason or think the materials present in our ecosystem is directly connected with our Eyes because to put psychological theories of if Freud into consideration our subconscious process of thinking is enriched by our conscious movements of eyes and reflections of what is imprinted on it. Therefore, if we can change how we see, then our own world can change like a flick, because if we do so the way we think also commutes beyond framed finger-rings!

Inking And Inspiring!

Inspiration in a general way refers to be motivated by anything or anyone. Psychologically, inspiration and inking in interconnected and interlinked. Both functions as complementary to each other, yet, can separately shine though. Inspiration is often the key source to work towards any goal! Even the worst situation inspires one to rise…unknown of humongous circumstances; inspiration has often influenced many great personalities to hanker on impossible things declared by the rest. Hope and inspiration also has a great bond- one assists the other to rise. Inspiration can source out of many things- any cultural diasporas, any specifically messaged films, any personality, any situational crisis or advantage, etcetera. However, there is a blur line of difference between 'inspiration' and 'aspiration', and one must not confuse between them as both of these terms are frequently and interchangeably utilized in premises of writing. 'Aspiration' is the hope or target to achieve a goal, while 'inspiration' is the mentally influenced or motivated state to work towards the effort needed to achieve the goal. Both are quite similar yet distinctively different. Inspiration drawn out of visual experiences often impacts the psychology more than other formats of the same. For, in general, memories acquired through abstract yet tangible materials often have resulted in productive outcomes of creative reflections in any arena. Even absence functions in the similar pattern, because often an absence yields in the question of 'why'; thereby involving one's thought in the process of finding the answer. Now, relation of writing or inking with inspiration has culminated so many things on which I just touched right now. Inking is the result of inspiration indeed but to be precise along with inspiration it is also the result of experiences both good and bad. Inking is also the result of knowledge mingling with inspiration. Inking is also the reflection of the desire to bring about a change, to portray few instances of complexities which goes unheard, to amplify few suppressed new which through printed forms get the avenue of circulation and flow! But somewhere, for every such incidents to take place we need that spark, that we call as inspiration- the result of which is even this piece which the readers will read!

The Juxtaposition of Hope and Fear

Fear and Hope are complimentary friends and foes of each other! We desire for hope because we are paranoid of something or the other. Often friction has resulted in sparking; however, such sparks often churn out of one's psychological voice that has been prolonged suppressed.

The Voice of Mind, are the reasons, why we write?

The Voice of Mind; A hyphenated phrase in fright,

The Voice of Mind, is a friend of the self in dark times?

The Voice of Mind- thus never fumbles,

When heart is emptied, and dear ones are away!

But have we ever though the reason why we are often afraid? Why fathoms of unanswerable interrogations have always marked our dawns and dusks like a rotational pattern of clock? No, we do not, because we either find the solution for our fright or try to remote it out from our sight. Hope only builds on attempts. If we are not the critical thinkers of our own tough, growth of Hanker is a difficult lot! Hence foundation here demands few words. Now, our crucial collapsing of fear and hope is frequently visible in the demands we tightly grope! The needs we present and require and the fear that we will be deprived from that results in the birth of those voices which screams to have what they need- I have a world too is a desired phrase often articulated in protest just to cope with a hope of peace in that world of Mine!

Immortal terms always has meant and guarded our notions to the usual meaning- something which do not dies, rather which live forever. But 'immortal' is every living beings who dies, why? They are not immortal because they die, they are so because the living life dies and not the being. The being is that inner, abstract self which scientifically yet superstitiously we refer as the 'spirit' lives through and after the death of the flesh and blood being. Now, here I am not talking about any paranormal activities. My main point comes, that, this 'abstract' self continues to live within the remaining people who knew the person who died; it lives through memories, through teachings, through habits, through love, through ideologies, through sharing. So, if I wish not to restrict the meaning of 'immortal' to the only domain of those who lives forever physically, then it includes people who even live in form of memories, relations, works like the great writers, etcetera. However, my meaning is also just not that! Immortal can be all our feelings, our perceptions, our wonderings, our existence too! Now, while exploring life and studies, theoretical knowledge has proclaimed that exploration can result in multifarious dimension of reality. It has portrayed how only while reconnaissance of various shades, can the diversity come to forefront. Therefore, if we are exploring or trying to analyze the 'exploration of immortality', the boundaries and horizon are blurring. To be more specific, there exists no such marked stoppage of this exploration. Immortal is thus every mortal matter. Beyond mortal/immortal rests such dimensions? Our knowledge being strategically binarized, we are forced to think within in the regular and convenient pattern of either this or that (this/that). A clear demarcation that is most often constructed by surrounding and ingrained as a "general process" through lifetime by individuals holds this fixed definition, indeed! So, exploring and trying to introduce selves with what plethora of meanings can be, will surely create a heuristic and hued spectrum of Immortal Explorations!

Suparna Roy

Drizzle-Open!

Drizzle or drizzling is the lightest, softest form of rain. It's open to all, but the way people will experience it is different, variant, layered. We all prefer to present our emotions in some form or other like through writing, speaking, drawing, studies, painting, etc. So here I will try to dribble my opinion about the term 'Open'.

Have we ever wondered how the use of every term varies with situation? A fixed meaning of any term doesn't exist, what exists is

relativity/associations/links. Feminism assisted in diagnosing the pathologies of culture which if described as a complex social apparatus dices the norms and regulations and is a stratified concept with hues that light up the disillusionment and dissent. Multiculturalism indeed has appreciated the difference in cultures but has also made avenues accessible to analyze it from queer perspectives. Within this complex spectrum of 'culture', terms and their meanings are altered and politicized. It has altering meanings in various spheres. Let's focus on society. How the term open has an ironical relation with our society.

Open is a term that acts as a compound word as it can be conjugated with any other term like 'open+minded' is 'open-minded'. In general, the term Open may be defined as means an idea or state that has flexible limitations and boundaries, that is susceptible to possibilities, recognitions and acceptance. But is it really the same? I don't think so for the present political scenario has made the term ironical. We have become regressively progressive; hence, we are openly close people. We are only open to what is easier to accept, we are only open to the mainstream of every form, our Constitution says we are 'open' to religion- secularism but here we are re-creating Hindutva, we are 'open' to voices-democracy, any one speaks against injustice, you are labeled as 'anti-national'! So when society says we have become modern, we are "open" to dibs, they actually mean we are open to what fits our idea of '*Sabhiyata*' and what is convenient for us to understand and accept, we are not open to "un-natural" things! Actually what's a society or a state or a country or a continent? These are few hypothetical terms which only exist because humans wanted them to exist. It's people that make up a society, state, country, and a continent. Being open is not a choice, but it's formulated. No one in our society can be open without 'power'. Therefore, its power which decides, what people can be open to even if they don't want to, what people don't open to, even if they want.

Body-shaming is another crucial and pertinent issue that echoes when school life gets reflected. It is very important to realize that a personality of a child grows not only from home but also from the various social groups, institutions we inculcate ourselves with. We don't even consider when we say someone- 'why are you having so low confidence?' 'Why can't you speak smartly?' and many other judging questions, without even realizing how the person or the recipient experiences about and after hearing it. Now, this 'body-shaming' is an important topic to talk about, particularly in today's society. But, before that, let's present few issues on culture, marginalization and society.

Feminism assisted in diagnosing the pathologies of culture which if described as a complex social apparatus dices the norms and regulations and is a stratified concept with hues that light up the disillusionment and dissent. Multiculturalism indeed has appreciated the difference in cultures but has also made avenues accessible to analyze it from queer perspectives. Culture and presentation of bodies dices each other into a complex fabricated network of tension that portrays incomplete and inaccurate characters. Our society has stated the ideal, the main, the center of everything that can define, identify, and visualize anybody of living beings. But, unfortunately amidst all such idealizations and modulations of the 'center' and the 'other', victims become those breathings, those voices, which recognizes not by these ideal statements of acknowledgement; rather, by what they feel about themselves and their surroundings. This handful of intonations echoes their experiences with situations, peoples, their own selves when identity and recognition is questioned. These vocalizations of a demand to understand the self and express it hovers the psyche and do not please 'Generalize' with the rest becomes the revolting phrase! Facing the self and the colors of it without subjugating it in the hands of mainstream dynamics is a very crucial phase of every single person who is deviant, who does not falls in the mainstream, who has demanded to live their lives on their own terms. Body shaming has also then become a branch of unconscious marginalization, the result of which is detrimental. We fumble to realize this very fact that variety is the essence of life.

So in our society power operates 'openness', making us (un) open to ourselves, to our voices, to our desires, dreams, identities and every other prospects. We hide because we are afraid; we are (un) open because we are powerless!

Conversing-Failure

Voices by- Teacher Rachel and eight graduate students

Rachel- Before we start talking about failure, let's know what is success? Success, by a very straight definition is associated only with career growth and a positive accomplishment of it. But success can also be a small child's able to speak the first letter. Minute things are categorized as normal while productive things are only recognized.

Student 1 (comments)-But it is equally important to espy the trivial matters like first purchase with the pocket money that is also a success. So, in this spectrum of success let's try to visualize the spectrums of failure and how we can still smile after failing!

Rachel- Right, so see, we are highly inspired by the thought- "Failure is the pillar of success." But do we actually believe in it? How important it is to believe thoughts that can assist dealing with depressions and every psychic struggle. It is also important to identify what is a failure and what is not so! Our culture has a complex derivative status that has created an 'ideal', a 'mainstream' for every minute issues of a human life- education, social life, religion, politics, identities, gender, love, etc and anyone deviating results in marginalization. Now, what we identify as failures, students?

Student 3- The definition of it varies diverges with age, class, caste, religion, gender, preferences, lifestyle, etc. Not being able to buy a five rupee confectionary maybe a failure for a very poor dalit woman who lives in a far remote area, while not being able to purchase an A-line dress of two thousand bucks maybe is a failure for one who lives in a metropolitan city. For some not being able to achieve the targeted aim in graduation result is a failure and for some not being able to crack a government job. For some failure is unsuccessful research work and for some incomplete world tour. So, failures distinguishably is interlinked with one's desire and amount of importance that person conveys towards a particular matter, and that can be anything which for the world's sake maybe the most frivolous. So for all to be able to face Failure with strength, we don't need famous sayings, but just small 'spaces' of our own and a little acceptance of existence and the spectrum of prospects. We need to include the possibilities of failing and not fix a specific failure category. Then only, it will result in more growth and less suicide hopefully!

Student 6- Ma'am, I want to share a real life experience- Back in 2018, when I completed my graduation on English Honours from Calcutta University, I pathetically scored worst in one of my honours paper, I qualified, my degree sustained because of the remaining marks and percentages of the previous years. Now, this wasn't supposed to happen, I was good in the first two years, I scored first class in the remaining three papers in my final year, then what happened to the one. Studies are important to me, it has been the only way, avenue, through which I realized I can escape, grow, fight, and have a voice. Therefore, I was shattered, depressed, I gave RTI for my paper but the time consumed was immense, I was not able to get admission for Master Degree in universities, etc. And finally when I got admission in Kalyani University after cracking the entrance exam in the second list, my review result was not out yet. But I wanted to know why was that, why I scored so, many questions hovered my head, but what 'other's said- this is just a small part of life, I have not faced any big failure, Admission happened *na*? That's all! Graduation result, failed in one honours paper, is not any matter, ignore and move on, she is making extra scene, what will she do with high degrees, etc comments were on plate. Education was my world, it was important for me and I feel that's enough, I increased my marks by twenty, it stood a second class marks from failed marks, and that was important for me, that fight was my success and after that I never bothered how other's view what my failure is! I am still paranoid of such mishaps in my career but I am more strong now because I see my failure's value as only mine, and no one can comprehend why it is a failure and neither great sayings will suffice the state of mind the.

Rachel- That's really heart wrenching! So could I make myself and the idea of failure clear?

Students (all)- Yes ma'am.

Rachel- So, what's it then?

Together all students- Failure is what you think is it, and go on fighting no matter wherever you start for it!

Does "Ideal" Exist? - Let's Be Open

Is this a question to entice one, was asked by the youth in rage! In the rat's race we involve ourselves, what matters is actually the 'secret'. Being first, or rising up earlier in comparison with others of your age is someone's desire; while, few feels theirs is nothing great in this; although, handful of others are quite struck between what they actually want? The problem is from our childhood we are not allowed to focus on what we actually like, we are not even provided with the opportunity to understand or realize our preferences. From our childhood we are just conditioned to become the "ideal", which perhaps is no one! But this bitter fact is never brought to the forefront and we the "idealization of the ideals" in every spheres of our life unfortunately goes on! The "ideals" are constructed and immense effort is made to preserve them through generations, so that people aim not become what they want, but aspire to reflect only the "ideals". In our effort to become like the "ideals" we forget our colors, our desires, our language, our sense of admiration, and our preferences. Everything gets mold under the ingrained construction of admiring the "ideals". Therefore,

Let's stop establishing one, omitting rest,
Let's stop becoming the 'one', and not the best,
It's important to consider what your heart desires-
Even, if that is hated by others.
Of what use is 'idealization'?
If it 'grey's' the power of individualization-
Let's chaperon the Fantasy of being the Real now,
Because, if not today, then oblivion will embrace our frame and brow!

Rhythm of a Minute Success

It was long back,
When the broken hopes smiled again-
It was long back,
When thoughts were jovial again-

Journeys creates moments,
Which are difficult to forget,
But they are the reason,
Why we thrust again.

Hopes were shattered,
When the steps were taken,

But 'that moment' of ratification-
Can never be forgotten!

Leaving behind,
Is the way to move on?
Exploring oneself in new avenues-
Is an adore, you're born for!

So, decades may pass before 'that moment ' arrives,
Hankering may be 'grey' before 'that moment ' will smile,
But, flow with rhythm to know where it lies,
Because life furnishes 'that moment ' only once, not twice!

<u>Duality</u> *The need to 'Recognize' it!*

Words are players, in the vagabondage of Life
Words are all, to make a call
Words have paved, all identities in shape
To give Humans the taste; Of Loss and Success!
Same were the terms- God and Devil-
Dwelling in the hearts of every human being,

Humans differentiated between them,
Loving the one and making the other hate.
As just two sides of the same coin-
Both God and Devil join,
Hands in hands they co-create,
All the existing binaries of good and bad!
To ignore Devil is to unaccept failure,
To ignore Devil is to water the fierce Desire,
To ignore the Devil is then to be selfless,
To ignore the Devil is then to live a life of Hell.
Only thinking of God can give you strength,
But the sense of competition comes from Hate
The Devil helps to create this craze-
While God says never do 'slap' others!
God assists to build the empire of truth,
But the value of which does not exist without a Lie-
God assists to build the sphere of Love,
But the value of which does not exists without Hate,
Now, if we only believe God and goodness then-
God has built all humans alike,
Why then differentiate between them?
God has loved all equally,
Why bargain with identity then?

God has sheltered all evenly,
Why then gender/sex/sexuality 'unsheltered' them?
God has welcomed everyone,
Why then caste and religion separate them?
So when we talk of God and Devil-
Let's not discrete them,
For society is made of dual combinations,
Where both rules as just and fair,
Where options no longer stay,
To opt the one and not the other-
Let's no longer sunder them,
For both exist in none other than Humans!

Apocalyptic Catastrophe-

A hyphenated jest!

Meanings of the two differs a bit,
One is minute and the other is fiercely horrific.
Duality dwells in whatever we say,
Like 'everything will be good' also has layers of rays-

'Everything will be good' is a form of hope,

'Everything will be good' is a disastrous trope,
For the phrase is used politically with smile-
Rising in anticipation with failed motives behind;

What brawn life can provide?
If the hope is shattered,
In the syntactical ambiguousness-
That situation has to offer!

'Everything will be good' is a shelter for heart
'Every will be good' can amass all impacted slots
Yet, 'Everything will be good' is a know 'sympathy'
Because the world lacks in felt empathy.

So experiences of 'Everything will be good' can be God's grace,
But can also exist in the form of dismantled dismay!

Society And Humans: A Reflection From Marginalized Perspectives.

Being a believer of post-stucturalist queer feminism, I think society has built an intricately fragmented and complex relationship/link with human beings and their individualities. Society runs on a strategically binarized format of identities and recognitions; hence, a mainstream, an ideal, an universalization, an 'umbrellaness' occurs in terms of everything outside the categorized boxes of gender, caste, sex, sexuality, religion, beliefs, ideologies, dialects, geo-locations, education, political policies, etc. From the perspective of immensely oppressed communities, I perceive that Feminism assisted in diagnosing the pathologies of culture which if described as a complex social apparatus dices the norms and regulations and is a stratified concept with hues that light up the disillusionment and dissent. Multiculturalism indeed has appreciated the difference in cultures but has also made avenues accessible to analyze it from queer perspectives. Identity and our skirmish in finding its appropriate nature have often pressurized the psychic nature of humans, particularly women. To be precise the struggling of marginalized identities is more toilsome in comparison to the 'centered' identities. In this phallocentric society the 'white-cis-phallus' is the centre and the remaining becomes the 'other'. Marginalization is a chain of events taking place in a society to create certain restrictions for few and power for the rest. Gender and Sexuality is not a concept to be 'inherently related'. Few things society has constructed to establish power dynamics- 'sexuality' as the assumption that everyone is "naturally" heterosexual. The remaining sexualities are not even considered as designations to be included while identifying human beings. Gender is a complex operative spectrum in a society, that functions in accordance to the numerous power dynamics operating with hunger of establishing themselves, of which patriarchy and feminism are the two powers that deals intensively with Gender. Lastly from caste's view, I feel, the subject, 'I' or 'we' in the identity equation, involves some element of choice, however limited. The concept of identity encompasses some notion of human agency; an idea that we can have some control in constructing our own identities. There are, of course, constraints which may lie in the external world, where material and social factors may limit the degree of agency which individuals may have. In this regard, we recognize how our stratified society has pushed and cramped the voices and the 'question of identity' of the Dalits.

Our society has stated the ideal, the main, the center of everything that can define, identify, and visualize anybody of living beings. But, unfortunately amidst all such idealizations and modulations of the 'center' and the 'other', victims become those breathings, those voices, which recognizes not by these ideal statements of acknowledgement; rather, by what they 'Feel' about themselves and their surroundings. This handful of intonations echoes their experiences with situations, peoples, their own selves when identity and recognition is questioned. These vocalizations say- 'Feel Me', and do not please 'Generalize' with the rest! This term 'Feel Me' is a very crucial phrase of every single person who is deviant, who does not falls in the mainstream, who has demanded to live their lives on their own terms. Have we ever felt to give few seconds of thought on our relational dynamics with our parents, our friends, partner/partners, close people, gossip people, and many other categories of persons who exist within our circle of life? Just like our social structure which run to establish commonalities and universality, sometimes, in some situations, on someday, this reflection of 'Feel Me' was omitted in our relational equations that existed or exits or will exist with people in our vivacity! It is not so hard to accept and prioritize this 'Feel Me' essence of a human being. We are often paranoid to experience this 'Feel Me' section of our lives because we are motivated by the fact that if this section is not a representation of what society has constructed to be the "ideal", maybe then I will be an 'Outcast'! Often, we do not converse regarding this section of 'Feel Me' with our parents, and near or dear ones like our partners, because we before expressing assume that the recipients will not be able to comprehend what I actually feel or what exactly I am experiencing now; they will only perceive and analyze me from their 'normative view' only. Hence, we control ourselves, we restrict ourselves from opening, accepting and experiencing, because somewhere we try to adjust and fit ourselves into the mainstream of constructed 'normalcy'. If we can do this our entire lives, it is fine; or else, we suffer, we break, we commit suicide, etcetera. 'Feel Me' is that essential part of our psyche which needs recognition from both the self and the others, but more importantly the self so that we can aspire with positivity. Hence, currently, the crucial thing which needs attention and transcendence is how we experience and feel our inner selves, how we recognize us through layers of comprehensions and not how 'generalize' statements shadows our 'Feel Me' to create US as them, as others and not the way we want US to be!!!

Pastels-Sexuality and Sexism

Patriarchy, if regarded as a constantly mutating drug resisting virus, then Feminism is an antidote to it. Stevie Jackson and Jackie Jones regarded in her article- *Contemporary Feminist Theory* that "The concepts of gender and sexuality as a highly ambiguous term, as a point of reference" (Jackson, 131, ch-10). Gender and Sexuality are two most complexly designed, culturally constructed and ambiguously interrelated terms used within the spectrum of Feminism that considers "sex" as an operative term to theorize its deconstructive cultural perspectives. Sexuality is not with whom we have sex rather it determines towards whom we are sexually attracted. But as Judith Butler said in *Gender Trouble* (1990), "sex" is not "natural"; sex (male/female) is seen to cause gender (masculine-men/ feminine- woman) which then is seen as a kind of continuum. The identity of what a "woman" is gets trapped in the supposed links between 'sex' and 'gender' to be inherently related and 'culturally' bound. Sexism more clearly means holding prejudice based on sex/gender and in our society it is done not only against 'women' but against all who is not *cis white upper-caste 'Men'*! To know of sexism it is important to know Sexuality, hence tried providing a little glimpses prior to discussing it! *Regulating Sexuality results in practice of sexism*, why? This is perhaps because of the Power, which has organized our "neat and clean" culture and society specifying a mainstream! If this Sexism behavior is not followed who will be the master and the slave, who the ruler and the ruled, who will order and who will follow, who will be free and who will e marginalized. If Sexism goes, Equality will exist, and that then will be immensely difficult for the Power to control bodies and make them work based on a format. Therefore, Sexism is taught, it is cultivated, it is maintained to dominate all and centre the 'one'!

An Idea On Feminism- Demanded Comment For Generation!

Simone De Beauvoir wrote that "the first time we see a woman take up her pen in defense of her sex"1, was Christine de Pizan who wrote Epitre au Dieu d'Amour (Epistle to the God of Love) in the 15th century. Feminism has altered predominant perspectives in a wide range of areas within western society, ranging from culture to law. Feminism, if considered a hermeneutical device which is a methodology for interpreting texts, it has always focused on the vast spectrum of marginalization in India, which is perhaps so intricately designed, that when it gets unfold; its spectrum reflects all those wailing lives which gets veiled by this intricate design of culture, power and aesthetics. Feminism assisted in diagnosing the pathologies of culture which if described as a complex social apparatus dices the norms and regulations and is a stratified concept with hues that light up the disillusionment and dissent. Multiculturalism indeed has appreciated the difference in cultures but has also made avenues accessible to analyze it from queer perspectives. Culture and presentation of women dices each other into a complex fabricated network of tension that portrays incomplete and inaccurate female characters. Women, as patriarchy defines them are only those with 'vaginas' and the 'intersectionality' is completely essentialized for 'identity' is only defined in parameter to 'body' and 'sex'. Gender and Sexuality are two most complexly designed, culturally constructed and ambiguously inter-related terms used within the spectrum of Feminism that considers sex as an operative term to theorize its deconstructive cultural perspectives. Feminism stands for 'inclusivity' that can act as a core for equality. Now it has become a norm to establish a person's identity based on only a single aspect of them, of which 'sexual identity' acts as a marker for all bodies(lesbians, gays, LGBTQ, man, woman, sex workers, dalits, etc). Sexuality has however remained as a medium of power and politics to control and produce resulting in creations of identities and maintaining an inherent link between Gender and Sexuality. But it is important to realize sexuality is not with whom we have sex rather it determines towards whom we are sexually attracted. It has been a "norm" to connect one's sexuality with their Gender and establish that as "naturally built". The dichotomy of 'penis/vagina' over years has linked itself to make/female understanding of bodies. However sexuality becomes more complex because it draws the 'desire' of a human body into consideration and when it does so it establishes an inherent link between sex and gender and desire. But as Judith Butler said in *Gender Trouble* (1990), "sex" is not "natural"; sex (male/female) is seen to cause gender (masculine- men/ feminine- woman) which then is seen as a kind of continuum. Butler emphasizes the fact that identity is free floating and not connected to one's 'essence rather performance'. As Mary McIntosh in her article- *Gender Trouble: Feminism and Subversion of Identity* said, "The way forward, instead, involves recognizing that gender attributes are performative rather than expressive" (McIntosh, 114). Desire or sexuality then becomes 'free-floating' and not connected to one's Gender/Sex. The problem arises when the society determines the connectivity and tries to establish the coherence between sex/gender/desire by presenting a human body with 'vagina' is bound to become a 'woman' and 'desire' a man confirming the heterosexuality and following it as the "ideal norm". Perhaps this "ideal norm" makes any "body" trying to deviate from the" legitimate couple, with its regular sexuality" (Foucault, 38) was a victim of patriarchy and as what Michel Foucault said in *The History of Sexuality* (1976) that "The legitimate couple, with its regular sexuality had more right to discretion. It tended to function as a norm, one that was stricter, perhaps but quieter" (Foucault, 38). Butler deconstructs this inherent connection and the 'compulsory order' of sex/gender/desire by stating that it is not sex that leads to gender and that leads to desire rather it is the 'mis-pre-understanding' which originates from one's "normative" desire, meaning heterosexuality is "norm", so a "man" has to have a "natural" phallus stating that it is desire that leads to gender that leads to sex- "If the immutable character of sex is contested, perhaps this construct called "sex" is a s culturally constructed as gender; indeed, perhaps it was always already gender, with the consequence that the distinction between sex and gender turns out to be no distinction at all" (Butler, 9-10). Thus the term Feminism can be used to describe a political, cultural or economic movement which at first aimed at establishing equal rights and legal protection for women and then gradually included all 'subaltern', marginalized voices. The theory of feminism together with post-structuralism and deconstruction has allowed us to include and 'play' with gender roles and identities rather than excluding and fixing it. Post-structuralist feminist theory in the field of literature has allowed us to deconstruct many literary texts and bring out 'what a literary text can mean' rather than the inherent meaning assumed to be present already, thereby making literature intersectional, reflective, interpretative and hence a spectrum, a sequence of thoughts, a journey through which the reader is able to make the 'illusive' world associated with reality. Feminism involves political and sociological theories concerned with issues of suppressed voices and 'marked bodies' resulted in production of works Gender Trouble where Butler indeed presents the feminist revaluation of 'drag' and promotes unity between feminists and gay movements. We can refer to Adrienne Rich's essay, *Compulsory Heterosexuality and Lesbian Existence,* where she mentions how lesbians were obliterated from literature and even from the mainstream feminist movement. She argues that society has made Heterosexuality "natural" so that it can be used as a violent political device to render women in a subordinate situation. Women are psychologically conditioned to think that they need to get a man to be sexually satisfied. They are restricted from enjoying the comfort of their own body with the same sex body. Lesbian motherhood is presented as inappropriate which forces women to accept heterosexuality as "natural" and obligatory and thereby fails to understand female sexual bonding is the only way that women can experience women identification. Therefore Feminism has demonstrated a welcome political turn and a journey without destination.

Suparna Roy

Stories From India

Being a bit systematic defining Politics in terms of what Wikipedia notes, stands as the set of activities that are associated with making decisions in groups, or other forms of power relations between individuals, such as the distribution of resources or status. It may be used positively in the context of a "political solution" which is compromising and non-violent or descriptively as "the art or science of government", but also often carries a negative connotation. Now, the present political scenario of India to make a 'simple' comment is quite similar to a Turkish proverb used by Paulo Coelho in his twitter comment that - 'The forest was shrinking but the trees kept voting for axe, for the axe was clever and convinced the trees that because his handle was made of wood he was one of them'. The reason for including this proverb is I somewhere feel we are the 'trees' and supporting the AXE! We can see how the promises of Anti-Romeo law, throbbing echoes of Hathras's case, the Farmer's Protest is reflecting the immensely patriarchal policies of centering and marginalizing human bodies; yet, the responses from our "educated" lot is indeed surprising. Acknowledging the very fact that our Indian society is a 'brahminical' one, hierarchies are inevitable. India's political scenario is regressively progressive. The rich are getting richer and the poor, poorer.

Politics or '*Rajniti*' is a spectrum. Our politics is nothing like the definition written in our constitution. I am not in the favor of any party nether am I demeaning one, I am just saying about the system, the realities which I can see.

Our Constitution believes in Democracy

Practice of it makes us 'anti-national'

Leaders' shouts in secularity

But creating Hindutva as unity!

We are always in search of 'new' faces

Maybe, that's why our political scenario is so perplexed.

Education is politicized

Hence humans dehumanized!

Neither I am a poet nor can I write poetry, it was just a small attempt to present few complexly designed issues. How a feministic view does then helps us to decode the current political agenda? Apparently Feminism recognizes while Patriarchy recognizes to obliterate. Feminism is also a politics but Feminism has assisted in diagnosing the pathologies of culture which if described as a complex social apparatus dices the norms and regulations and is a stratified concept with hues that light up the disillusionment and dissent. Multiculturalism indeed has appreciated the difference in cultures but has also made avenues accessible to analyze it from queer perspectives. It has 'spectrumized' how Culture and presentation of Gender and Sexuality dices each other into a complex fabricated network of tension that portrays incomplete and inaccurate characters as everyone except for the 'mainstream men'. Politics is one of the many channels through which power flows and our politics has always allowed the operation of marginalizing power regimes like gender, caste, religion, class, geo-location, sexuality, sex, etc intertwine with each other in a manner that if one raises voice to demand their right from a particular point, fails to realize that oppression has oppressed them from other spectrums too. Here, our politics assists us and separates us from the rest of the points, hence rules by dividing, we even fumble to realize that.

Pandemic opened virtual access on every platform, the present politics ceased and limited them by passing the protocol that virtual conferences before presenting international wise will have to take permission to represent anything that highlights India's privacy, well the underlying meaning is oppression. A very intense political link is their between now and the British Rule of 200 years- 1756-1947. I only feel that the present politics is only enriching itself at the cost of not all Indians but "anti-nationals". Education can be a boon and a curse both. If we get education including possibilities we get to know many, but if it's modified to create and organize a particular class and group then English Missionaries of the British Rule is nothing different from Hindutva of present times. So supporting the present political scenario and voting for them should also make us aware that we unconsciously or consciously are supporting the marginalization based on-

- Gender, where the centre is only 'upper-caste, Hindu, heterosexual male' and rest 'sorts' of men, all 'forms' of women, LGBTQIA++, are the peripheral others! Gender is only one branch among the numerous branches of oppression, most securely intermingled with caste, religion, sexuality, sex, class, location, language, and race, and etc!
- Marginalization based on caste where if a dalit boy is refrained from entering temple, we say nothing and if a dalit woman is raped by Brahmin CM '*ka beta*', we say nothing.
- Marginalization based on class, where farmer's have no life
- Marginalization based on colour where Fair&Lovely is the only line
- Marginalization based on Education where knowledge accessibilities are limited and modified
- Marginalization on personal freedom where speaking against the wrong will receive Hitler's response.
- Marginalization based on every minute right of humans that makes them 'smile'.

Letting these stories flow is important

About the Author

Suparna Roy

Suparna Roy is an Assistant Professor of English (Dept of Applied Sciences and Humanities) at Global Institute of Management and Technology, and an Independent Researcher. She has qualified CTET and has obtained her Master's in English Literature (2020) and completed her B. ED in 2022.

Besides her academic qualifications, she has a first-class in French intermediate language learning (2019), and experience teaching for more than three years in various fields. She is deeply engaged in the research of South Asian studies focusing on Gender and Literature from an intersectional perspective.

She has more than 20 publications (journals, chapters in books, pre-prints, magazines, e-newspaper, book), and 30+ presentations until that date.

She has also completed one research project on Queer Identities and Gender Intersectionality; one under Think India Tribal Rights Forum. She was also selected for Doctoral Research Program under Summer Sexuality Fellowship 2022 at California Institute of Integrated Studies *(https://professorpennyharvey.weebly.com/ciis-sexuality-summer-research-fellowship)* under Dr. Penny Harvey and Dr. Michelle Marzullo. She is also a selected researcher in the En-gender group - *https://engenderacademia.wordpress.com/south-asian-studies/*.

www.ingramcontent.com/pod-product-compliance
Lightning Source LLC
LaVergne TN
LVHW041637070526
838199LV00052B/3424